Stars
& Poppy Seeds

You never fail until you stop trying.

Albert Einstein

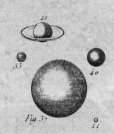

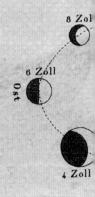

Romana Romanyshyn & Andriy Lesiv

Stars
& Poppy Seeds

TATE

Flora

Dad

Mum

Flora loved to count more than anything else in the world.
Her parents were famous mathematicians, and numbers, figures and
all kinds of formulae had filled her life ever since she was small.
While other children counted sheep to fall asleep,
Flora counted all of the animals in the world.
She even counted sea cows, elephants and platypuses.

$418/6$

$72\dots$

14^2

$c^2 = a^2 + b^2$

≈ 5600897000

$2 \times 2 = 4$

$\dfrac{50}{2}$

Flora counted everything around her.
She counted poppy seeds, grains of rice,
the polka dots on her new red dress, the pearls on
her mum's necklace and the letters in her dad's book.

For fun, Flora made a portrait of her bunny,
Pythagoras, from sixty-five tiny poppy seeds.
She also created a portrait of the neighbour's cat,
Newton, using only black peppercorns.

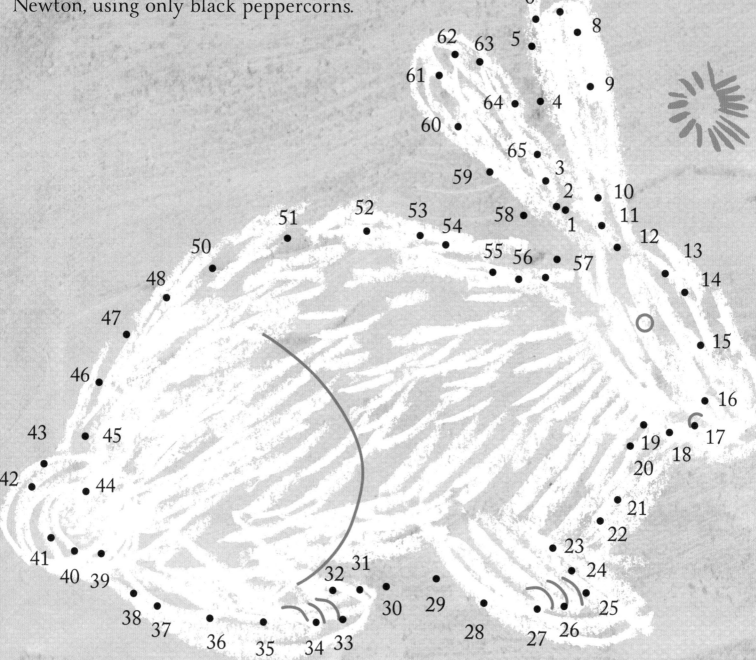

While walking in the park, Flora counted the leaves, the dandelions,
the stones and the ants scurrying all over the place. She loved to count the
buttons on the coats of passers-by, and even the holes in those buttons.
She counted bricks in a medieval tower. Then she counted fifteen fir trees
at the end of the street, and seven more in front of the fountain.

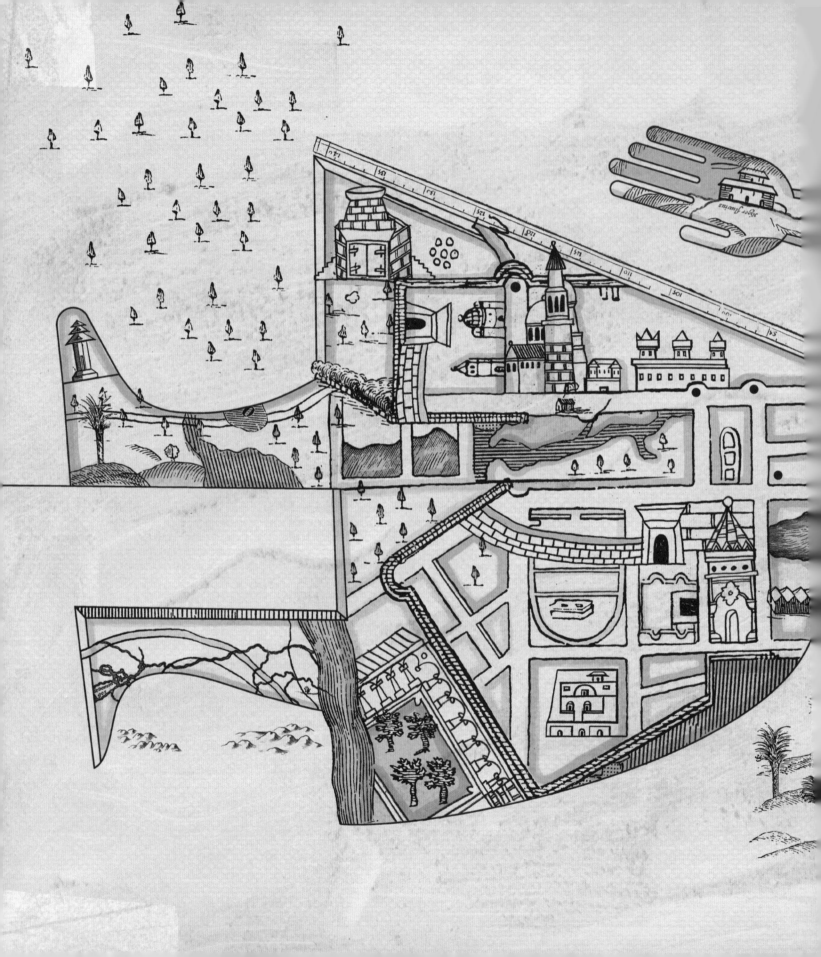

Sometimes, Flora imagined that the city was lost in the middle of a desert.
Then, she would try to think of how many grains of sand there were
in all of the deserts and beaches in the world.

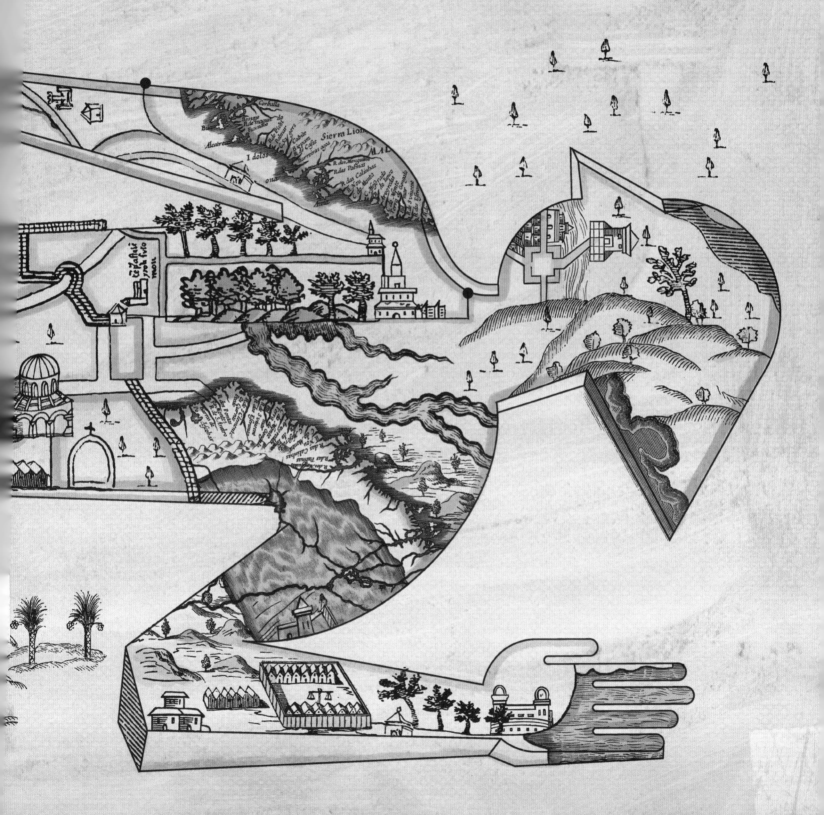

One day, as Flora walked home
through the labyrinth of streets,
she suddenly found herself near a lake.

Her mind began to whirl.

How many droplets of water
were there in the lake?

How many were there in the sea?

And how many
in all of the world's oceans?

That evening, Flora looked with delight through a telescope at the starry sky above. Of course, she tried to count all of the stars. Her room was filled with models of the solar system, maps of the sky and a whole collection of meteorites.

The stars reminded Flora of the seeds she had
fed to the birds in the park last summer.
Looking up at the bright, shinning lights of the Milky Way,
Flora started to try to count all of the stars.

Fig.18

Flora realised there were
so many stars in the night sky
that not even all of the numbers she knew
would be enough to count them.

There were millions. There were billions, even trillions of stars . . .

Flora was determined to count the stars.
She tried the complicated formulae and equations
her parent's had taught her, but it was no good.
It was an impossible task.
Disappointed, Flora turned to her mum and asked,
"Why can't I count all of the stars in the sky?
I know so many numbers, formulae and equations,
but even they aren't enough!"

$$E = \frac{m \cdot v^2}{2}$$

$$10 \times 8 \frac{x}{y} = \cot^2 \alpha$$

$$58340078?$$

$$2489$$

$$100000000\}$$

$$+$$

$$1000000 \}$$

$$247.9322$$

$$1258367200$$

$$530047 \times 64489 = ?$$

$$2 \times 48354 \quad \overline{x + 2y}$$

Flora's mum pulled her close and said,
"You can accomplish anything you set your mind to.
Every task, even the most complicated, begins the same way:
with one step. If you take small steps,
you can achieve even your biggest dreams.

One, two, three . . ."

Flora smiled. She counted all of the animals in the world
(even the sea cows, elephants and platypuses,)
then she fell asleep and dreamed of stars.
Millions and billions and trillions of them . . .

Fun with figures

You could fit 1 million earths into the sun!

Scientists believe that our universe was created 13.5 billion years ago with the Big Bang!

The largest number with a name is called a "googolplex", which is written as the number 1 followed by a googol zeros. (A googol is 1 followed by 100 zeros.)

The sun is around 4.6 billion years old!

As of June 2018, 561 people have gone to space, but only twelve people have walked on the moon!

Our solar system lies roughly 30,000 light years from the centre of the Milky Way.

The sun is our nearest star. It has a mass 330,000 times that of earth.

There are 9,096 stars visible to the naked eye in the night sky!

Four is the only number in the English language that is spelled with the same number of letters as the number itself.

Stars are usually between one and ten billions years old.

Famous mathematicians

Pythagoras (580-c.500)

Pythagoras was a Greek philosopher, mathematician and scientist who is best known for his work in mathematics, geometry, music and astronomy. Pythagoras' theorem is the theory that, in a right-angled triangle, the square of the hypotenuse (the longest side) is equal to the sum of the squares of the other two sides.

Sir Isaac Newton (1642-1727)

Sir Isaac Newton was a mathematician, astronomer, physicist and author. He is famous for outlining the three laws of physics, and for discovering gravity. He also discovered that light isn't white, but is actually made up of lots of different colours.

Ada Lovelace (1815-1852)

Ada Lovelace was a British mathematician and writer, who is regarded as the first computer programmer. She worked with Charles Babbage on the first "computer" and thought the machine could do more than just calculations - so she wrote an algorithm for the machine.

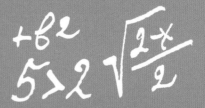

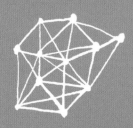

Albert Einstein (1879–1955)

Albert Einstein was a German physicist. He developed the theory of relativity and an equation for mass-energy equivalence ($E=MC^2$). He won the Nobel Prize for Physics in 1921.

1 0 0

Katherine Johnson (1918–)

Katherine Johnson is an African-American mathematician who worked for NASA. She calculated the trajectories of space flights such as Apollo and the Space Shuttle programme. It is thanks to Katherine that humankind ended up on the moon!

86

Stephen Hawking (1942–2018)

Stephen Hawking was a British physicist, cosmologist and Lucasian Professor of Mathematics at the University of Cambridge. He studied the relationship between space, time and black holes, and and published his famous book *A Brief History of Time* in 1988.

3474829

$72+53c=\sqrt{a^2+b^2}$

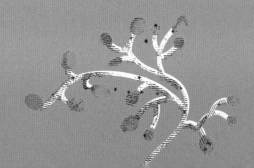

Explore the world of Mathematics!

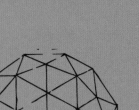
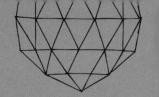

Armagh Observatory & Planetarium
Armagh, Northern Ireland
armaghplanet.com

The National Museum of Computing
Milton Keynes, United Kingdom
tnmoc.org

The National Museum of Mathematics
New York, USA
momath.org

National Space Centre, United Kingdom
Leicester, United Kingdom
spacecentre.co.uk

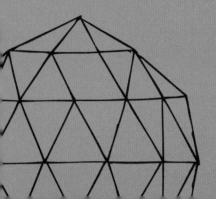

Royal Observatory
London, United Kingdom
rmg.co.uk/royal-observatory

The Garden of Archimedes
Florence, Italy
web.math.unifi.it/archimede/archimede_NEW_inglese/

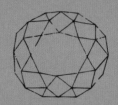

Jodrell Bank Discovery Centre
Cheshire, United Kingdom
jodrellbank.net

Mathematikum
Glessen, Germany
mathematikum.de

Science Museum
London, United Kingdom
sciencemuseum.org.uk

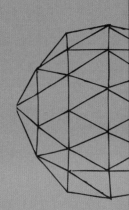

Sydney Observatory
Sydney, Australia
maas.museum/sydney-observatory

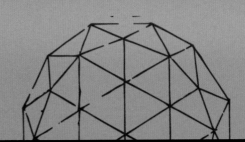

First published in 2019 by order of the Tate Trustees
by Tate Publishing, a division of Tate Enterprises Ltd, Millbank, London SW1P 4RG
www.tate.org.uk/publishing

Text and illustrations © Romana Romanyshyn and Andriy Lesiv 2014
English translation © Oksana Lushchevska 2019
Information pages © Tate Publishing 2019

Originally published in 2014 under the title *Зірки і макові зернята*
by Vydavnytstvo Staroho Leva (The Old Lion Publishing House), Lviv, Ukraine
This edition © Tate 2019

A catalogue record for this book is available from the British Library

ISBN 978 1 84976 620 3

Distributed in the United States and Canada by ABRAMS, New York
Library of Congress Control Number applied for

Colour reproduction by DL Imaging, London
Printed and bound in China by C&C Offset Printing Co., Ltd